SO-ARL-180

EX LIBRIS Friends of
Lake County Public Library

3 3113 01204 1663

GRANNY, LET ME IN!

Adapted by Jill Barnes
Story and Illustrations by Wakiko Sato

◳ᓱᓭ GARRETT EDUCATIONAL CORPORATION

LAKE COUNTY PUBLIC LIBRARY

What a hot day!
The sun was high in the sky.

Granny wanted a cool place.
She took her book and said,
"It's cool in the shade
under the tree. I'll read there."

Granny sat down
under the tree.
She began to read.

A rabbit hopped along.
It wanted to be in
the cool shade, too.

"Granny, Granny, let me in,"
the rabbit said.

Granny smiled at the rabbit.
"There's room for you," she said.

Granny read, and
the rabbit felt cool
and sleepy.

But along came a cat.
It wanted to cool off.
The day was so hot!

"Let me sit in the shade,"
the cat said. "Granny, Granny,
let me in, too."

Granny and the rabbit said,
"Yes, there's room for you."

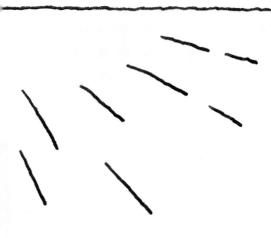

Soon a dog trotted along.
It saw Granny and the rabbit
and the cat under the tree.

"Granny, Granny, let me stay
in the shade," the dog begged.

"Oh, this feels so cool,"
the dog said, wagging its tail.

Granny and the rabbit and
the cat were not so happy.
But they made room
for the dog.

Granny was reading, and
the rabbit, the cat, and
the dog napped when. . .
     along
     came
      a snake
       looking
        for a
      cool
       spot.

Nobody wanted the snake.
But the snake didn't care.
It was so cool in the shade!

The snake tried to make friends.
Granny stopped reading.
The rabbit, the cat, and the dog
wanted the snake to go away.

Just then a fox came by.

The fox didn't ask
if there was room.

The fox crowded in, and
nobody at all liked that.

Granny tried to read.
The animals fell asleep.
So, only Granny saw what
was coming —
        a big furry bear.

Now there was real
trouble.

The bear did not ask
to sit in the shade.
It just pushed everyone
out of the way.

The sun was not so high
in the sky, and there was
more shade under the tree.
The bear closed its eyes,
and Granny shut her book.

Then, here came an elephant!

"There has to be room for ME,"
the elephant said.

He pushed Granny and the rabbit,
the cat and dog, the snake, the bear,
and the fox, out of his way.

The elephant sat down,
and the other animals
crowded together.

But there was no place
in the shade
for Granny.

All the animals
were alseep.

Granny made a plan.
She found a little branch.

"I'll tickle that elephant
and make it go away,"
she thought.

The elephant **sneezed**.

"**Eeeee!**" cried Granny.

The tree's leaves were
blown off, and —
the elephant was still there.

"Look what
you have done,"
Granny cried.
"**Go away!**"

Now Granny was alone.
"There's just enough shade
for me," she said.
        And she read until
            the sun went down.

Edited by Caroline Rubin

U.S.A. text copyright© 1990
by Garrett Educational Corporation

GRANNY, LET ME IN! by Wakiko Sato
Copyright© 1987 by Wakiko Sato
Originally published in 1987 in Japanese,
under the title "CHOTTO IRETE"
by KAISEI-SHA PUBLISHING CO., LTD.,
English translation rights arranged with
KAISEI-SHA PUBLISHING CO., LTD.,
through Japan Foreign-Rights Centre

All rights reserved. Published by
Garrett Educational Corporation
130 E. 13th Street, Ada, Oklahoma 74820

Manufactured in the United States of America

Library of Congress Cataloging-in-Publication Data
Barnes, Jill.
Granny, let me in/adapted by Jill Barnes:
story and illustrations by Wakiko Sato.

    p.   cm.
    Summary: Wanting a cool place to read, Granny
sits in the shade of a tree - only to be joined by
animal after animal until there is no room for
herself.
ISBN 0-944483-82-8
[1. Grandmothers - Fiction. 2. Animals - Fiction
3. Trees - Fiction.]
I. Sato, Wakiko. Chotto irete.
II. Title.
PZ7.B2623Gr 1990   90-37752
[E] - dc20   CIP
                     AC

Ex-Library: Friends of
Lake County Public Library

JUV P BARN   CL
Barnes, Jill.
Granny, let me in

X

LAKE COUNTY PUBLIC LIBRARY
INDIANA

AD	FF	MU
AV	GR	NC
BO	HI	SC
NOV 2 4 '92 CL	HO	SJ
DY	LS	CN L

THIS BOOK IS RENEWABLE BY PHONE OR IN PERSON IF THERE IS NO RESERVE
WAITING OR FINE DUE.

LCP #0390